Rookie reader

Go-With Words

Written by
Bonnie Dobkin

Illustrated by
Tom Payne

Children's Press®
A Division of Grolier Publishing
New York • London • Hong Kong • Sydney
Danbury, Connecticut

For the Group: Josh, Jason, Jessica, Elana, Sara, Jon, Scott,
Eric, Ron, and Bradley
—B. D.

Reading Consultants
Linda Cornwell
Coordinator of School Quality and Professional Improvement
(Indiana State Teachers Association)

Katharine A. Kane
Education Consultant
(Retired, San Diego County Office of Education and San Diego State Universi

Visit Children's Press® on the Internet at:
http://publishing.grolier.com

Library of Congress Cataloging-in-Publication Data
Dobkin, Bonnie.
     Go-with words / by Bonnie Dobkin; illustrated by Tom Payne.
          p. cm. — (Rookie reader)
     Summary: Rhyming text presents examples of words that go together, such as "top
with bottom, down goes with up," "fat goes with skinny, short goes with long," and "nig
goes with moon and day goes with sun."
     ISBN 0-516-22031-4 (lib. bdg.)   0-516-27048-6 (pbk.)
     1. English language—Synonyms and antonyms Juvenile literature. [1. English
language—Synonyms and antonyms.] I. Payne, Tom, 1958– ill. II. Title. III. Series.
PE1591.D595 2000   99-33427
428.1—dc21   CIP

Cat goes with kitten.
Dog goes with pup.

Top goes with bottom.

Down goes with up.

Fat goes with skinny.

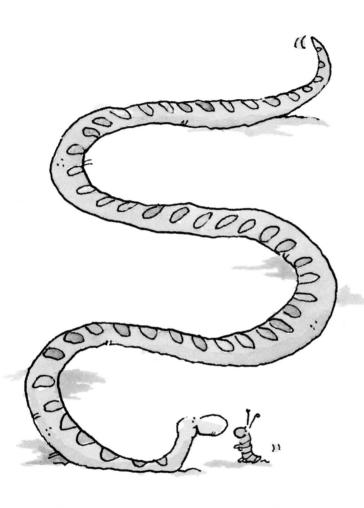

Short goes with long.

Read goes with story

and listen with song.

A joke makes you laugh.
A cut makes you cry.

You clap with your hands.
You wink with your eye.

Page goes with book

and brick goes with wall.

Square goes with box

and round goes with ball.

Letters mean reading.

Numbers mean math.

Bad means a time-out.

Dirty means bath.

Night goes with moon

and day goes with sun.

Hand goes in glove

and hot dog in bun.

A bat hits a ball.

A hammer hits nails.

Trains have cabooses.

Some monkeys have tails.

Eggs go in cartons

and cans on a shelf.

Now think of more
go-with words by yourself.

Word List (82 words)

a	cry	hot	now	sun
and	cut	in	numbers	tails
bad	day	joke	of	think
ball	dirty	kitten	on	time
bat	dog	laugh	out	top
bath	down	letters	page	trains
book	eggs	listen	pup	up
bottom	eye	long	read	wall
box	fat	makes	reading	wink
brick	glove	math	round	with
bun	go	mean	shelf	words
by	goes	means	short	you
cabooses	hammer	monkeys	skinny	your
cans	hand	moon	some	yourself
cartons	hands	more	song	
cat	have	nails	square	
clap	hits	night	story	

About the Author

Bonnie Dobkin grew up in Morton Grove, Illinois, and later received a degree in education from the University of Illinois. She has worked as a high-school teacher and executive editor in educational publishing. For story ideas, Bonnie relies on her three sons, Bryan, Michael, and Kevin, and her husband, Jeff. When not writing, Bonnie focuses on her other interests—music, community theater, and chocolate. She lives in Arlington Heights, Illinois.

About the Illustrator

Tom Payne has been a humorous illustrator for a very long time. His work has appeared in all sorts of books and magazines. He commutes into his studio, which he shares with some other "arty" people, in Albany, New York, from his home in the nearby Helderberg Mountains. He lives with his wife, Anne, and his son, Thomas.